to: ....

from: ....

All Creatures Great and Small

Cecil F. Alexander

sourcebooks
jabberwocky

PRECIOUS
MOMENTS

All things bright and beautiful,

all creatures great and small,

all things wise and wonderful,

the Lord God made them all.

Each little flower that opens,

each little bird that sings,

He made their glowing colors,
He made their tiny wings.

The purple-headed mountains,

the river running by,

the sunset and the morning

that brightens up the sky.

The cold wind in the winter,

the pleasant summer sun,

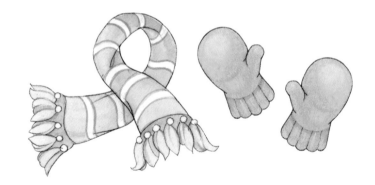

the ripe fruits in the garden,

He made them, every one.

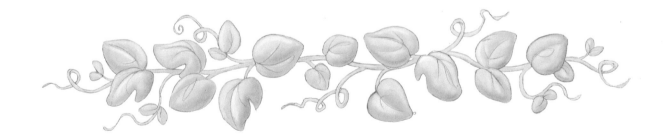

The tall trees in the greenwood,

the meadows where we play,

the rushes by the water,

we gather every day.

He gave us eyes to see them,

and lips that we might tell

how great is God Almighty,

who has made all things well.

All things bright and beautiful,

all creatures great and small,

all things wise and wonderful,

the Lord God made them all.

Cover and internal design © 2019 by Sourcebooks, Inc.
Cover and internal images © Precious Moments
Original text by Cecil F. Alexander, 1848

Published by Sourcebooks Jabberwocky, an imprint of Sourcebooks, Inc.
P.O. Box 4410, Naperville, Illinois 60567-4410
(630) 961-3900
Fax: (630) 961-2168
sourcebooks.com

Source of Production: Leo Paper, Heshan City, Guangdong Province, China
Date of Production: January 2019
Run Number: 5013845

Printed and bound in China.

LEO 10 9 8 7 6 5 4 3 2 1